Low Carb Coo[k] UK

CW00411527

Healthy and Easy-to-follow Recipes with Colored Pictures + 14 Days Meal-Plan

By **Grace Martin**

TABLE OF CONTENTS

INTRODUCTION

WHAT IS A LOW-CARB DIET?

Low-carbohydrate diets refer to diets that contain very few carbohydrates compared to an average diet.

Let's start with some basic principles, there are 3 main macro-nutrients:
- Carbohydrates
- Proteins
- Fats

A low-carb diet aims to avoid the assumption of high-carb foods, particularly foods like wheat, bran, oats, potatoes, and ultra-processed foods.

As we aim to lower the carbs intake, we need to focus our diet on the 2 other categories of macronutrients: proteins and fats. This will be done by eating foods such as meats, fish, dairy, fruits, vegetables, nuts, and seeds.

Obviously, we won't cut out all the carbohydrates intake from our diet, but we are going to reduce it. Just to get a general idea, low-carb diets require you to eat fewer than 130 grams of carbohydrates each day, and they will come only from healthy sources.

At the end of the book, there is a 14 Days Meal-Plan that we have created as a guideline to help you follow the diet; feel free to ignore it or apply changes to it to suit your needs.

WHO SHOULD STARTS A LOW-CARB DIET?

First of all, it is correct to say that a low-carb diet is not suitable for everyone, and before starting a new diet (this suits every diet, not only a low-carb one), you should consult your doctor or dietitian beforehand. Each person is unique, and your needs may be different from someone else.

However, it has been found that low-carb diets are highly beneficial for many people that can be divided into the following groups:

- People who suffer from type 1 diabetes
- People who are looking to lose weight
- People who have an upcoming long-distance athletic event
- People with high blood pressure or high blood cholesterol levels

THE BENEFITS OF A LOW-CARB DIET

Reduce the daily carbohydrates intake implies a lot of health benefits, including the ones below:

APPETITE DECREASE

Hunger can be difficult to deal with if you're trying to lose weight or cut out processed food and it is one of the main reasons why people give up on their diets after just a couple of weeks. Fortunately, in a low-carb diet, the assumption of high quantities of protein and fat helps you fight the hunger pangs due to the natural feeling of satiety that these macro-nutrients can provide.

WEIGHT LOSS BOOST

Removing starchy foods from your diet is a very efficient way to lose weight because it leads to a calorie deficit.

Furthermore, those who follow a low-carb diet lose weight quicker than those who eat a high-carb, low-fat diet because carbohydrates tend to hold onto water in their body. Reducing your carb intake implies that your body carries less water, which basically results in weight loss.

LOWER BLOOD PRESSURE

High blood pressure, known medically as hypertension, is a significant risk factor for a range of different health conditions, including heart disease, stroke, type 2 diabetes, and kidney disease. Eating a low-carb diet can reduce your blood pressure and, therefore, reduce your risk of developing these diseases.

BLOOD CHOLESTEROL LEVELS IMPROVEMENT

The consumption of simple sugars can increase blood triglyceride levels. Low-carb diets help to decrease the levels of triglycerides in your blood, which can also decrease your risk of developing heart disease.

Additionally, a low carbohydrate intake can decrease the levels of low-density lipoproteins (LDLs) in your blood. LDLs are the 'bad' cholesterol because they can increase plaque build-up in your arteries, leading to a higher risk of atherosclerosis and heart disease.

Low-carb diets can also increase the levels of high-density lipoproteins (HDLs) in your blood. HDLs are the 'good' cholesterol that have the opposite effect to LDLs and lower the risk of plaque buildup.

WHAT SHOULD YOU EAT AND WHAT NOT

Since this diet aims to reduce carbohydrates, certain foods are very suitable for our purpose. Those are foods high in proteins and healthy fats, and in this section, we have listed some of them:

- Red Meat and Poultry: chicken, turkey, grass-fed beef, pork, lamb, and duck
- Fish: salmon, cod, haddock, white fish, and tuna
- Fruits: apples, oranges, strawberries, blueberries, pears, peaches
- Vegetables: almost every vegetable is appropriate, aim to include lots of broccoli, cauliflower, carrots, sprouts, spinach, and kale in your diet
- Dairy: eggs, cheese, yoghurt, and milk
- Non: dairy alternatives – tofu, tempeh, dairy-free cheese, dairy-free yoghurts, and various nut milks
- Nuts and seeds: almonds, cashews, walnuts, pistachios, brazil nuts, hazelnuts, sunflower seeds, pumpkin seeds, chia seeds
- Oils: olive oil, coconut oil, fish oil, grass-fed butter

There are also some foods that you can consume but in lower quantities, like:

- Legumes: lentils, kidney beans, white beans, black beans, and pinto beans
- Starchy vegetables: white potatoes, sweet potatoes, parsnips, turnips, and swede
- Grains: brown rice, wholemeal pasta, oats, quinoa, and buckwheat
- Dark chocolate: should contains at least 75% cocoa

On the other hand, there are certain foods that you should avoid during this diet. As the suggested amount of carb intake per day is around 130 g, it is a good practice to spread them throughout the whole day instead of eating them in a single meal. This will grant you more sustained energy and will help you to feel fuller and more satiated. Unfortunately, this implies that high carbohydrate foods will almost disappear from your diet.

We have listed some of the key foods to avoid during this diet:

- Refined grains: wheat, barley, rye, pasta, bread, cereal

- Sugar: processed snacks (sweetened chocolate, candy, ice cream, cookies), pastries, honey, agave, and sweetened soft drinks or sodas
- Trans fats: hydrogenated or partially hydrogenated oils
- Starchy vegetables: white potatoes, sweet potatoes, and parsnips

CHAPTER 1: BREAKFAST

VEGAN PANCAKES

10 minutes

20 minutes

4

INGREDIENTS

- 300g frozen red berries
- 100ml Alpro Yogurt Alternative
- Lemon, juice and zest
- 2tsp baking powder
- 100g wholemeal flour
- 125g plain flour
- 120g mashed banana
- 300ml Alpro Almond Unsweetened drink, chilled
- Peanut butter
- Cooking oil

DIRECTIONS

1. Cook the berries and lemon juice/zest in a saucepan over low heat until it reaches the consistency of a compote. Set aside and keep warm.
2. Mix the baking powder and flours and create a hole in the middle. Mix the mashed banana and Alpro Almond Unsweetened drink in a pitcher and then pour it into the hole created in the flour. Stir until the mixture is smooth.
3. Heat some oil in a frying pan and pour 2 tablespoons of batter (each pancake is around 2 tablespoon of batter). When bubbles begin to appear on the top of each pancake, flip it over. Repeat until all the batter is used up.
4. Gently heat the peanut butter to melt it. Serve a stack of 3-4 pancakes per person and top with the hot compote, a spoonful of peanut butter and Alpro *Yogurt Alternative*.

Nutrition: 348kcal, 7.7g Fat, 53.9g Carbohydrate, 7.1g Fibre, 11.2g Protein

CARAMELIZED BANANA BREAD WAFFLES

15 minutes

35 minutes

4

INGREDIENTS

- 100g porridge oats
- 1 tsp baking powder
- ½ tsp ground cinnamon
- 1 large egg, lightly beaten
- 150ml buttermilk
- 3 large ripe bananas, two mashed and one cut into thick diagonal slices
- 2 tsp sunflower oil
- 20g walnut halves
- ½ tbsp maple syrup
- 75g Total 0% fat Greek natural yogurt
- 2 tbsp double cream
- 1 tsp vanilla bean paste

DIRECTIONS

1. Preheat the oven to 180°C/fan 160°C/gas mark 4. Mix together the porridge oats, baking powder and cinnamon. Whisk in the egg and buttermilk, then the mashed bananas, until combined.
2. Grease a silicone 4 rectangle waffle mold with 1 tsp oil and place on to a tray. Pour in the mixture evenly then transfer to your oven and bake for 30-35 minutes until it is cooked through(it should be a little crispy on the edges).
3. Meanwhile, heat a medium non-stick frying over a medium heat until hot. Add the walnuts and toss in the pan for 3-4 minutes until toasted. Remove from the pan, roughly crush and set aside.
4. Toss the sliced banana in the maple syrup. Heat the remaining oil in the same frying pan over a low-medium heat and add the banana. Cook, turning frequently, for 5 minutes until the banana becomes golden brown and crispy on the edges. Remove from the heat and set aside.
5. Add the yogurt and double cream along with the vanilla paste to a small bowl and beat with an electric whisk until whipped into soft peaks. Serve the whipped yogurt with the waffles, caramelised bananas and walnuts.

Nutrition: 317kcal, 11.6g Fat, 39.6g Carbohydrate, 4.3g Fibre, 10.7g Protein

KEFIR PANCAKES

10 minutes

15 minutes

4

INGREDIENTS

- 200g plain flour
- 1 tsp baking powder
- 1 tsp vanilla extract
- 2 eggs, beaten
- 500ml kefir
- 2 tbsp runny honey
- 4 tsp sunflower oil
- 320g frozen red berry mix

DIRECTIONS

1. In a bowl, add the flour, baking powder, and a pinch of salt. Stir to mix everything together and form a well in the center. In a separate bowl, combine the vanilla extract, eggs, kefir and honey, then pour in the dry ingredients. Gradually combine with a whisk and refrigerate for 10 minutes to let the mixture rest.
2. Add 1 tablespoon sunflower oil to a large nonstick skillet over medium heat and pour a quarter of the batter into it. Cook each side until small bubbles form on the surface (around 2-3 minutes), then flip and cook for another 2-3 minutes.
3. Let the pancakes rest in a plate and cover with foil. Add 1 tablespoon of oil each time you empty the pan and repeat until all the batter has been cooked.
4. Meanwhile, place the berries in a skillet and cook over low heat for 5 to 6 minutes (they should begin to break down). Serve the pancakes with the compote on top and a drizzle of honey.

Nutrition: 356kcal, 7.6g Fat, 57.1g Carbohydrate, 2.1g Fibre, 13.1g Protein

AVOCADO TOAST

10 minutes

2 minutes

1

INGREDIENTS

- 1 avocado
- 2 slices keto bread
- Juice 1 lemon
- ½ tsp black pepper

DIRECTIONS

1. Remove the skin and the pit from the avocado and slice.
2. Place the keto bread in the toaster and cook to your desired crispness.
3. When the toast is ready, add the avocado slices and squirt the lemon juice on top. Add a sprinkle of black pepper and serve while the bread is still hot.

Nutrition: 289 kcal, 12 g Fat, 10 g Carbohydrates, 7 g Protein

SCRAMBLED EGGS WITH PORCINI AND PROSCIUTTO

10 minutes

15 minutes

6

INGREDIENTS

- 25 g dried porcini mushrooms
- a few rosemary sprigs, plus extra to serve
- 20 g butter
- 12 large eggs, lightly beaten and seasoned
- 1 small handful of grated parmesan, plus extra to serve
- 12 slices sourdough bread
- 6 slices of prosciutto

DIRECTIONS

1. Soak dried porcini in plenty of hot water until softened. Drain, rinse well and check for grit, then coarsely chop.
2. Heat a large nonstick skillet and melt half the butter. When it has stopped sizzling, add the beaten eggs and lower the heat. Slowly cook the mixture, stirring occasionally, for 8 to 10 minutes. When it is almost cooked but still creamy, remove from the heat and add the chopped porcini, the rest of the butter, and the handful of cheese. Stir lightly and check the seasoning.
3. Griddle or toast the sourdough slices, then rub them with the rosemary sprigs to flavor the bread. Spread the scrambled eggs on the plates and add the ham. Sprinkle with more Parmesan cheese and serve with the rosemary bruschetta and more rosemary for garnish.

Nutrition: 422 kcal, 20.0g Fat, 29.5g Carbohydrate, 208.0g Fibre, 29.7g Protein

BAKED EGG AVOCADOS

5 minutes

15 minutes

4

INGREDIENTS

- 4 eggs
- 2 avocados
- 55 g of bacon
- 20 g of cheddar cheese
- 1 tomato
- 1 teaspoon of basil
- Pinch of salt
- Pinch of pepper
- 2 tablespoons of chives

DIRECTIONS

1. Preheat your oven to 200 degrees C.
2. Cut your avocados in half lengthwise and scoop out the pits. Leave the skins on.
3. Get out a baking sheet and place the avocado halves on it, facing up.
4. Use a spoon to enlarge the hole left by the pit. You can use this flesh up in other recipes if you choose.
5. Top each avocado with an egg, bacon, slices of tomato, and a little of cheddar cheese.
6. Bake the avocado in the oven for 15 minutes, or until egg yolks are cooked.
7. Chop your herbs and sprinkle them across the avocados to serve.

Nutrition: 369 kcal, 31.4 g Fat, 10.5 g Carbohydrate, 7.2 g Fibre, 14.1 g Protein

BACON AND EGG ROLLS

10 minutes

10 minutes

4

INGREDIENTS

- 6 eggs, beaten
- 2 tbsp milk (any type)
- ½ tsp garlic powder
- ¼ tsp black pepper
- 1 tbsp salted butter
- 12 slices bacon
- 80 g of cheddar cheese, grated

DIRECTIONS

1. Beat the eggs, milk, garlic powder and pepper in a large bowl until combined.
2. Heat the butter in a skillet and once it is melted, pour in the egg mixture, and cook for 3-4 minutes, stirring regularly to form a scramble.
3. Place the bacon slices flat on a chopping board and spread half of the cheddar cheese evenly across the bottom third of each slice. Top the cheese with half of the egg scramble.
4. Repeat with the remaining halves of cheese and egg scramble until all of the ingredients have been used.
5. Carefully roll up the bacon slices, keeping the cheese and egg mixture tightly inside.
6. Add the bacon rolls to the hot skillet and cook for 5 minutes of either side until the bacon turns dark and crispy.
7. Serve immediately.

Nutrition: 313 kcal, 25 g Fat, 9 g Carbohydrates, 17 g Protein

17

GOJI BERRY AND CHIA SEED BOWL

35 minutes

0 minutes

2

INGREDIENTS

- 370ml Alpro original coconut fresh drink
- 75ml coconut milk yogurt alternative, natural
- 20g goji berries
- 40g chia seeds
- 10g Naturya organic maca powder
- 100g frozen blackberries
- 1 Pear
- 20g pomegranate seeds
- 10g Naturya organic cocoa nibs

DIRECTIONS

1. If using frozen blackberries, remove the necessary amount from the freezer and let them sit in a bowl to begin thawing; if using fresh berries, skip this step and add them only at the end of the recipe.
2. Place the chia seeds, goji berries, and coconut milk in a pitcher and combine well with a spoon. Let stand for 5-7 minutes, then stir the mixture again to make sure all the chia seeds are mixed in. Let it sit for another 20-25 minutes to allow the chia seeds to absorb the milk.
3. Once the chia seeds and goji berries have absorbed the milk and have doubled in size, stir in the coconut yogurt and maca powder.
4. While you are waiting for the chia and goji berries, around the last 5 minutes of soaking, wash the pear, remove the stem and core, and cut it into chunks.
5. Pour the chia, goji berry and coconut mixture into two small bowls.
6. Add the blackberries, pear and pomegranate, then sprinkle with the raw cocoa nibs.

Nutrition: 382 kcal, 20.0g Fat, 34.0g Carbohydrate, 18.0g Fibre, 7.8g Protein

REFRIED BEANS WITH POACHED EGGS

5 minutes

25 minutes

2

INGREDIENTS

- 1 medium onion, chopped
- 1 tsp vegetable oil
- 1 x 308g carton black beans
- 1 red chilli
- ½ jar of Loyd Grossman tomato & chilli
- 350g pasta sauce
- 100g smoked bacon lardons
- ½ tsp smoked paprika
- 10 cherry tomatoes, halved
- 1 tbsp olive oil
- ½ lime, juice only
- 1 tbsp chopped coriander leaves
- ½ medium red onion, chopped
- 4 eggs
- 1 tbsp white vinegar/ white wine vinegar/ cider vinegar
- 1 pinch salt
- 1 pinch pepper

DIRECTIONS

1. Mix the cherry tomatoes, red onion, olive oil, lime juice, and cilantro leaves to prepare the sauce. You can season with salt and pepper to taste and then set aside.

2. Heat vegetable oil in a large nonstick skillet and cook the onion for 2-3 minutes. At this point add the bacon lardons and let them cook for 5 minutes (the bacon should be ready and the onion soft).

3. Season with chili and paprika and cook for 30 seconds. Add beans and pasta sauce; heat and cook for 2-3 minutes. Remove from heat and mash beans a bit with a wooden spoon or potato masher. Set aside in the pan.

4. Bring a large pot of water to a boil and add the vinegar. Gently crack the eggs into the pan and cook them for about 3 minutes. Remove them with a spoon and let them drain on a sheet of kitchen paper.

5. Return the beans to the heat and reheat them. Once hot, arrange on two plates and top with the eggs and sauce.

Nutrition: 588kcal, 37.3g Fat, 23.8g Carbohydrate, 10.6g Fibre, 34.1g Protein

SCRAMBLED EGGS AND SMOKED SALMON

3 minutes

5 minutes

1

INGREDIENTS

- 2 eggs
- 50 g of smoked salmon
- Pinch of dill
- ½ tablespoon of butter
- Pinch of salt

DIRECTIONS

1. Melt the butter in a small skillet above medium heat. Tear up the smoked salmon and toss it into the pan to warm.
2. Whisk the eggs into a cup until they are frothy and airy.
3. Pour the eggs into the pan and stir, constantly scraping the mixture into the centre of the pan and moving it around so that it cooks evenly and the salmon mixes through it.
4. Serve topped with dill and a touch of salt.

Nutrition: 243 kcal, 17 g Fat, 0.8 g Carbohydrate, 0 g Fibre, 21.5 g Protein

LOW-CARB BREAKFAST WAFFLES

5 minutes

5 minutes

4

INGREDIENTS

For the waffles:

- 6 eggs
- 2 bananas, mashed
- 2 tbsp peanut butter or almond butter
- 3 tbsp wholemeal flour
- ½ tsp ground cinnamon

For the toppings:

- ½ tbsp cashew butter
- ½ tbsp coconut butter
- 4 medium strawberries
- 1 tsp honey or maple syrup

DIRECTIONS

1. Heat a waffle iron until hot.
2. Meanwhile, mix all of the waffle Ingredients in a large bowl until they form a smooth and consistent mixture
3. Coat the waffle iron with cooking spray and pour 1/4 of the batter into the iron.
4. Cook for a few minutes until golden.
5. Repeat this a further three times to create four delicious waffles.
6. Serve warm with the cashew butter, coconut butter, strawberries, and honey on top.

Nutrition: 359 kcal, 17 g Fat,15 g Carbohydrates, 19 g Protein

BANANA BREAD

5 minutes

45 minutes

6

INGREDIENTS

- 50 g of almond flour
- 3 bananas
- 3 eggs
- 120 g of almond butter
- 1 tablespoon of cinnamon
- 1 teaspoon of vanilla extract
- 1 teaspoon of baking soda
- 1 teaspoon of baking powder
- 4 tablespoons of melted butter

DIRECTIONS

1. Preheat your oven to 230 degrees C.
2. In a bowl, mash your bananas thoroughly into a smooth mush.
3. Mix the almond butter into the bananas.
4. Melt the butter using a microwave or over the stove and then add it to the bowl.
5. Mix the eggs in the bowl together with the vanilla extract.
6. Add the almond flour, baking powder, baking soda, and cinnamon to the bowl and stir thoroughly.
7. Grease a loaf tin and pour the batter in, and then bake for 45 minutes.
8. Insert a toothpick to check that it comes out clean, if so take the banana bread out of the oven and let it rest for 10 minutes. Turn it out onto a cooling rack to finish cooling, and store in an airtight container.

Nutrition: 222 kcal, 15.2 g Fat, 17.3 g Carbohydrates, 3.3 g Fibre, 5.8 g Protein

STRAWBERRY AND AVOCADO SMOOTHIE

5 minutes

0 minutes

1

INGREDIENTS

- 200 g of strawberries
- 1 avocado
- 200 ml non-dairy milk (almond, cashew, hazelnut, soya, or oat)

DIRECTIONS

1. Clean the strawberries and chop them in half.
2. Peel the avocado and remove the pit. Chopped into small chunks.
3. Pulse all the ingredients into a blender or a food processor until they are fully combined.
4. Serve in a glass and enjoy!

Nutrition: 106 kcal, 12 g Fat, 6 g Carbohydrates, 10 g Protein,

KALE CHIPS

5 minutes

15 minutes

4

INGREDIENTS

- 200 g of kale
- 1 tbsp coconut oil
- 1 tsp chili powder
- 1 tsp cumin

DIRECTIONS

1. Preheat the oven to 200 °C and line a baking tray with parchment paper.
2. Rinse the kale and allow to dry. Tear into small pieces and discard the stems.
3. Place the kale in a mixing bowl and toss in the coconut oil and spices to coat.
4. Spread the kale evenly over the baking tray and bake in the oven for 15 minutes until crispy and brown.
5. Serve immediately.

Nutrition: 87 kcal, 5 g Fat, 5 g Carbohydrates, 3 g Protein

CHILI HOT DOGS

 15 minutes

 1 hour

 6

INGREDIENTS

- 1 tbsp olive oil
- 1 red onion, finely chopped
- 2 red peppers, sliced
- 500g 5% fat beef mince
- 2 tsp hot chili powder
- 1 tsp cumin
- 1 tsp paprika
- 500ml passata with onion and garlic
- 2 squares dark chocolate
- 410g tin red kidney beans, drained and thoroughly rinsed
- 250ml beef stock, made with 1 beef stock cube
- 600g sausages
- 6 white finger rolls
- 1 tbsp ketchup, to serve
- 1 tbsp mustard, to serve
- 1 red chili, finely sliced, to serve

DIRECTIONS

1. Heat some oil in a large pot, then add the onion. Cook for 2-3 minutes until it starts to sauté, then add the peppers. Cook for another 3-4 minutes (peppers should become tender).
2. Add the chili powder, cumin and paprika and stir, cooking for 1 minute. Place the mince in the pan and move it around, breaking it up with a wooden spoon. Cook for 3-4 minutes (should be browned all over).
3. Pour in the passata and broth. Bring to a gentle simmer and cook for 30 minutes.
4. Put the chocolate in a cup and melt it in the microwave (it should take around 30 seconds to melt). Add it to the chili along with the beans. Alternatively, you can add the chocolate pieces directly to the chili. Stir to combine everything, then simmer for another 15 minutes until the mixture has thickened slightly.
5. Meanwhile, cook sausages according to package directions; place sausages in rolls along with spoonfuls of chili. Serve with ketchup, mustard and sliced red chili.

Nutrition: 648 kcal, 32.3g Fat, 42.2g Carbohydrate, 9.5g Fibre, 42.5g Protein

ZA'ATAR AUBERGINE SANDWICHES

10 minutes

20 minutes

4

INGREDIENTS

- 4 tbsp olive oil
- 2 tsp za'atar
- 3 large aubergines, sliced lengthways
- 200g roasted red peppers, roughly chopped
- 250g mozzarella, thinly sliced
- 125g sundried tomatoes

DIRECTIONS

1. Preheat the oven to 200°C/fan 180°C/gas mark 6. Create a mixture by mixing the olive oil and za'atar and brush the eggplant slices on both sides with it. Heat a frying pan over high heat and sear the eggplant slices for one minute on each side until they begin to soften and show signs of the griddle. It is necessary to perform this operation in several rounds

2. Line up eight eggplant slices on a lightly greased baking sheet and top them with a layer of peppers, some mozzarella and sun-dried tomatoes. At this point place another 8 slices of eggplant so as to create sandwiches; Bake for 10 minutes, until the eggplant is soft and the cheese is stringy.

Nutrition: 399kcal, 31.6g Fat, 13.3g Carbohydrate, 1.8g Fibre, 14.4g Protein

SALMON, CHEDDAR, AND WATERCRESS SCONES

10 minutes

20 minutes

12

INGREDIENTS

- 300g self-raising flour, plus extra for dusting
- 1 tsp baking powder
- 120g smoked salmon
- 75g unsalted butter, diced
- 1 medium free-range egg, lightly beaten
- 1 tsp Dijon mustard
- 75g baby leaf watercress, washed and roughly chopped
- 150ml semi-skimmed milk
- 120g lighter soft cheese
- 75g mature Cheddar, grated

DIRECTIONS

1. Preheat the oven to 220°C/gas mark 7. In a large bowl, sift the flour and baking powder together. Add a pinch of salt, then rub in the butter with your fingertips (or combine in a food processor).
2. Create a well in the middle of the mixture and stir in the egg, milk, mustard, 50g cheddar and three quarters of the watercress. Bring the dough together with your hands and shape into a ball.
3. On a floured surface, roll out the dough to a 1½cm thickness. Cut 12 rounds with a 6-7cm fluted cutter (or small glass), gently re-rolling and using the trimmings. Place on a floured baking tray, leaving space between each. Scatter with the remaining Cheddar and bake for 10-15 minutes, until golden.
4. Cool the scones on a wire rack. To serve, top with the soft cheese and smoked salmon and garnish with the remaining watercress.

Nutrition: 202kcal, 10.6g Fat, 24.9g Carbohydrate, 1.1g Fibre, 11.7g Protein

TOMATO AND FETA SKEWERS

10 minutes

0 minutes

20 skewers

INGREDIENTS

- 20 Vittoria tomatoes
- 200g of barrel-aged feta, cut into 20 cubes
- 20 fresh basil leaves
- Balsamic vinegar, to drizzle
- Extra virgin olive oil, to drizzle

DIRECTIONS

1. Remove the tomatoes from the vine and wash. Halve and lay out the tomatoes, feta cubes and basil leaves on separate plates.
2. Build your skewers using cocktail sticks. Start with a tomato half, then add a folded basil leaf and a feta cube.
3. Arrange on a serving platter and, once complete, drizzle with the balsamic vinegar and olive oil and season to taste.

Nutrition: 37kcal, 2.9g Fat, 0.9g Carbohydrate, 0.0g Fibre, 1.7g Protein

EGG MAYONNAISE SANDWICH

2 minutes

8 minutes

4

INGREDIENTS

- 8 slices of wholemeal bread
- 80 g butter
- 4 free range eggs, hard boiled, chopped
- 2 tbsp mayonnaise
- 0.5 Romaine lettuce
- 4 apples

DIRECTIONS

1. Boil the eggs for 8 minutes.
2. Spread the bread slices with butter or vegetable spread.
3. In a bowl, mix the chopped, hard-boiled eggs with the mayonnaise, then spread on 4 of the bread slices. Top with lettuce hearts and the remaining bread, then cut into quarters.
4. Finish your lunch off with an apple each.

Nutrition: 311kcal, 14.6g Fat, 29.8g Carbohydrate, 6.1g Fibre, 12.0g Protein

CHOCOLATE PROTEIN SHAKE

5 minutes

0 minutes

1

INGREDIENTS

- 200 ml almond milk
- 1 scoop chocolate Protein powder
- 2 tbsp almond butter
- 1 tbsp cocoa powder
- 2 tsp stevia
- 2 tbsp chia seeds
- 1 tsp vanilla extract

DIRECTIONS

1. Place all of the ingredients into a blender or food processor.
2. Blend until a smooth and consistent mixture has formed.
3. Pour the Protein shake into a cup and enjoy!

Nutrition: 250 kcal, 16 g Fat, 8 g Carbohydrates, 26 g Protein

TANDOORI CHICKEN BURGERS

10 minutes

15 minutes

2

INGREDIENTS

- 2 garlic cloves, crushed
- 2cm piece ginger, grated
- 1 little gem lettuce, torn
- 2 tbsp tandoori spice paste
- 8 tbsp natural yogurt
- 2 large skinless chicken breast fillets
- 4 ciabatta rolls, halved
- 16g coriander, leaves picked
- 3-4 tbsp mango chutney, plus extra to serve
- 1 large tomato, sliced

DIRECTIONS

1. Mix together the garlic, ginger, spice paste, half the yogurt and some seasoning in a large bowl. Cut each chicken breast in half horizontally, then add to the marinade and mix. Cover and set aside for at least 15 minutes, or overnight in the fridge. Preheat the grill.
2. Transfer the chicken to a baking tray and grill for 10-12 minutes or until cooked through, turning halfway. Keep warm while you lightly toast the ciabatta buns.
3. Spread a little chutney on the base of each roll, then top with the tomato, lettuce and chicken. Add a dollop of the remaining yogurt and some coriander and serve with extra chutney for dipping.

Nutrition: 439kcal, 6.3g Fat, 57.2g Carbohydrate, 4.5g Fibre, 35.9g Protein

BAKED ORZO WITH GRAFFITI AUBERGINE

10 minutes

35 minutes

4

INGREDIENTS

- 375g orzo
- 1pt (568ml) chicken stock – using 1 Knorr chicken stock pot
- 112g (half) Spanish chorizo ring
- 1 graffiti aubergines
- 2 sweet pointed peppers
- 180g cherry tomatoes
- 1 large red onion
- 1 large garlic clove
- 6 sprigs fresh thyme
- Several fresh purple basil leaves
- 3 tbsp roasted red pepper pesto
- ½ tbsp extra virgin olive oil

DIRECTIONS

1. Pre-heat the oven to 220°C/ fan 200°c/ gas mark 7 and pop the kettle on to boil. Peel the skin off the chorizo and cut into rounds about ½cm wide. Chop the graffiti aubergines into small cubes around 1cm thick, slice the sweet pointed peppers into rounds about ½cm thick. Chop the red onion in half, peel and chop into large chucks around 2cm thick. The idea is to have slightly varying sizes for added texture, so don't feel you need to be exact here.

2. Add the chorizo to an oven-friendly pan, a cast iron shallow casserole dish works really well,and dry fry on the hob using medium-heat. Stir occasionally until the oils are released, this usually takes around 2-3 minutes. Then add the graffiti aubergines, sweet pointed peppers, onions and stir to coat in the chorizo oil. Add the tomatoes, still on the vine and transfer dish to the oven. Roast for 10 minutes.

3. Meanwhile mince the garlic and make up 1 pint (568ml) of chicken stock, set to one side. After the chorizo and vegetables have roasted for 10 minutes, take the dish out of the oven and place back on the hob using a low heat. Turn the oven down to 190C/ fan 170C/ gas mark 5.

4. Remove the tomatoes from the dish so you can give everything a good stir. Add the minced garlic, orzo and the red pesto. Let the orzo soak up the cooking oils and pesto for a moment, then add the stock. Place the tomatoes back on top. Put the dish back into the oven, covered with a lid and cook for 8 minutes.

5. After 8 minutes, take the dish out of the oven and fluff the orzo up with a fork (be sure to scrape the bottom of the pan to really mix everything). Stir through half a tbsp extra virgin olive and add back to the oven for a further 5 minutes un-covered.
6. After the final 5 minutes, check the orzo is cooked to your liking (slightly al dente works best). If it needs a couple more minutes or is looking too dry, add a splash of water (no more than 3 tablespoons) and place back in the oven un-covered until ready.
7. To serve, give the orzo a final fork through and scatter fresh thyme and purple basil leaves over the top for a fresh finish. Season with salt and pepper to taste.

Nutrition: 613kcal, 23.0g Fat, 75.0g Carbohydrate, 10.0g Fibre, 21.0g Protein

SEAFOOD STEW WITH PAPRIKA

10 minutes

50 minutes

4

INGREDIENTS

- 1 tbsp olive oil
- 600g diced swede and carrot
- 2 yellow peppers, sliced
- 1 red chilli, sliced
- 2 red onions, diced
- 2 tsp paprika
- 700ml chicken stock, made with 1 stock cube
- 390g carton chopped tomatoes
- 1 tbsp tomato pureé with garlic
- 180g raw king prawns
- 250g cod, cut into 2-3 cm pieces
- 2 limes, one squeezed and one cut into wedges
- 100g bag baby leaf spinach
- 1 bunch coriander, roughly chopped

DIRECTIONS

1. Take a large saucepan and heat oil over medium heat. Add the onions and season, then cook for 5 minutes or until softened. Add the swede and carrot and sauté on a low heat for 10 minutes.

2. Add the chilli, paprika, stock, chopped tomatoes and tomato pureé. Sauté for 5 minutes. Add the peppers and bring to the boil. Reduce the heat and simmer for 15 minutes.

3. Add the prawns and cod and place a lid on top of the pan. Cook for 5 minutes over a medium-high heat. Take off the heat and add the spinach. Allow it to wilt, stirring occasionally. Add the juice of one lime and sprinkle over the coriander. Serve with the lime wedges.

Nutrition: 276kcal, 5.1g Fat, 22.0g Carbohydrate, 9.7g Fibre, 30.7g Protein

SZECHUAN TUNA WITH SALAD

8 minutes

20 minutes

4

INGREDIENTS

- 1kg baby potatoes
- 2 cloves of garlic, finely chopped
- 3 tbsp rice vinegar
- 1 tsp whole Szechuan peppercorns, crushed
- 3 tbsp light soy sauce
- 200g trimmed mange tout, thinly sliced lengthways
- 200g radishes, trimmed and coarsely grated
- ½ cucumber, trimmed, halved, deseeded and cut into sticks
- 1 tbsp vegetable oil
- 400g tuna steaks

DIRECTIONS

1. Put the potatoes in a large pan, then cover with cold water and bring to the boil. Cook for 15 minutes, until tender. Drain and cut in half.

2. Meanwhile, mix together the garlic, 1 tbsp rice vinegar, the peppercorns and the soy sauce in a small bowl. Set aside.

3. Stir in the radish, mange tout and cucumber. Season with the remaining rice wine vinegar and then mix everything together.

4. Heat the oil in a large frying pan. Add the tuna steaks and cook them for 2 minutes, then turn them over. Pour in the Szechuan seasoning and continue to cook the tuna for another minute if you want it medium-cooked, or for another 2 to 3 minutes if you prefer it well done. Serve the tuna with the pan juices, potatoes, and salad on the side.

Nutrition: 365kcal, 5.4g Fat, 37.2g Carbohydrate, 8.0g Fibre, 37.8g Protein

CHICKEN FAJITA PASTA

| 10 minutes | 20 minutes | 4 |

INGREDIENTS

- 2 tsp smoked paprika
- 1 tsp chilli powder
- 1 tsp ground cumin
- ½ tsp cayenne pepper
- ¼ tsp garlic powder
- 460g chicken breasts, cut into strips
- 1½ tbsp olive oil
- 350g penne pasta
- 1 red onion, sliced
- 1 red pepper, deseeded and sliced
- 1 yellow pepper, deseeded and sliced
- 2 tbsp tomato puree
- 230g tomato salsa
- 150g low-fat sour cream
- 50g reduced-fat cheddar cheese, grated

DIRECTIONS

1. Form a mixture by combining smoked paprika, chili pepper, cumin, cayenne and garlic powder and then season half of the chicken pieces with it. Heat 1 tablespoon of oil in a large, deep skillet and cook the chicken for 5-6 minutes (it should be golden brown). Remove and set aside.
2. Meanwhile, cook the pasta according to package instructions. Once drained set aside, saving a little of the cooking water.
3. Heat the remaining oil in the skillet and sauté the onion with the remaining spice mixture for 3-4 minutes, until tender. Season with salt as desired and add the peppers, cooking them for another 3-4 minutes until softened.
4. Add the chicken to the skillet and the tomato puree. Cook for 2 minutes, then add the cooked pasta, sauce, and sour cream. Heat everything through, and if the sauce needs loosening, add a little of the pasta cooking water until the desired consistency is reached. Sprinkle with cheese to serve.

Nutrition: 620kcal, 13.8g Fat, 74.3g Carbohydrate, 7.7g Fibre, 45.9g Protein

SAUSAGE AND ROASTED VEGETABLE COUSCOUS

15 minutes

30 minutes

4

INGREDIENTS

- ½ butternut squash, peeled, deseeded and sliced
- 1 aubergine, washed and cut into bite-sized pieces
- 200g couscous
- 2 tbsp olive oil
- 8 extra-lean Cumberland sausages
- 2 tsp smoked paprika
- 3 classic round tomatoes, quartered
- 2 tbsp fresh flat-leaf parsley, washed and chopped

DIRECTIONS

1. Preheat the oven to 220°C/gas mark 7. Place the sausages, butternut squash and aubergine on a large baking tray in a single layer. Drizzle over the olive oil and sprinkle with smoked paprika, then roast in the oven for 15 minutes.

2. Turn the vegetables and sausages, add the tomatoes and roast for a further 10 minutes, until the vegetables are tender and lightly charred at the edges and the sausages are cooked through.

3. Meanwhile, place the couscous in a bowl (should be heatproof) and pour boiling water over it. The amount of water should be the same as the couscous, e.g. 1 cup couscous - 1 cup water. Let it stand for 5 minutes until the water has been absorbed by the couscous and stir occasionally.

4. Fluff up the couscous with a fork, then season with freshly ground black pepper and stir in the parsley. Cut the sausages into chunks and put in a large bowl. Add to the couscous with the roasted vegetables and any juices from the baking tray. Toss everything together, divide between 4 plates and serve.

Nutrition: 429kcal, 9.8g Fat, 55.2g Carbohydrate, 3.7g Fibre, 28.0g Protein

CHEDDAR AND LEEK CROQUETTES

 10 minutes

 20 minutes

 6 croquettes

INGREDIENTS

- 2 tbsp olive oil
- 3 leeks, washed and finely chopped
- 150g fresh breadcrumbs
- 50g mild cheddar, grated
- ½ bunch fresh chives, finely chopped
- 3 medium free-range eggs

DIRECTIONS

1. Heat 1 tbsp oil in a frying pan,then add the leeks and cook until softened. Tip the cooked leeks into a bowl with 100g breadcrumbs, the cheddar, chives and 2 eggs. Mix together well, then place the bowl in the freezer for 5 minutes.
2. Place the remaining breadcrumbs in a shallow dish. Put the remaining egg into another shallow dish and gently beat.
3. Take the mixture out of the freezer and shape into 6 large sausage shapes or 12 smaller ones. To breadcrumbs coat each sausage in egg and then in breadcrumbs.
4. Heat the remaining oil in a frying pan and, over a medium heat, fry the croquettes for 10 minutes until golden.

Nutrition: 207kcal, 9.5g Fat, 18.7g Carbohydrate, 3.4g Fibre, 9.9g Protein

GREEK LAMB WRAPS

5 minutes

12 minutes

4

INGREDIENTS

- 1 tbsp olive oil
- 1 red onion, finely sliced
- 300g cooked roast lamb, shredded
- 1 clove garlic, finely chopped
- 2 tsp dried mixed herbs
- 4 tortilla wraps
- ½ cucumber, chopped
- 335g salad
- 12 cherry tomatoes, chopped
- 230g tzatziki

DIRECTIONS

1. Heat the oil in a large frying pan and sauté the onion and garlic for 5 minutes until soft. Add the lamb and ½ the dried herbs, and stir-fry for 2 minutes, until warmed through.
2. Meanwhile, lay the tortillas out on to plates. Divide the salad, tomatoes and cucumber between the wraps and top with the lamb mixture. Sprinkle the remaining dried herbs over the tzatziki and serve on the side.

Nutrition: 496kcal, 22.0g Fat, 42.7g Carbohydrate, 3.5g Fibre, 30.2g Protein

JAMAICAN-STYLE COCONUT FISH PARCELS

8 minutes

30 minutes

4

INGREDIENTS

- 1 tbsp vegetable oil
- 1 onion, diced
- 1 red pepper, sliced
- 250ml coconut cream
- 1 yellow pepper, sliced
- 1 tbsp finely grated ginger
- 2 cloves garlic, crushed
- ½ tbsp finely chopped thyme leaves
- ½ tsp ground allspice
- Juice of ½ lime
- 1 tbsp soft light brown sugar
- 1 scotch bonnet chilli, finely chopped
- 4 salmon fillets

DIRECTIONS

1. Heat the oil in a frying pan over medium heat, then add the onion. After 5 minutes, add the peppers and cook for another 5-8 minutes (they should soften). Add the chili, ginger, garlic, thyme and allspice and cook for 2 minutes. Add the coconut cream with a splash of water so that it is diluted and simmer for 2 minutes. Remove from heat and add the lime juice and sugar, then season to taste.
2. Prepare four packets by laying out a large sheet of foil with a sheet of wax paper on top (you may need to cut it to make it about the same size as the foil). Place a salmon fillet on each, then lift the sides slightly and divide the coconut sauce between each portion. Crush the sides to create a parcel, but leave enough room for the fish to steam.
3. Place each parcel on a hot barbecue or griddle for 8-10 minutes, until the fish is just cooked through. Open the parcels and serve.

Nutrition: 466kcal, 34.5g Fat, 11.1g Carbohydrate, 3.0g Fibre, 26.3g Protein

ROAST VEGETABLE FRITTATA WITH MACKEREL

 10 minutes

 55 minutes

 4

INGREDIENTS

- 1 red onion, cut into wedges
- 1 yellow pepper, deseeded and cut into thin slices
- 1 red pepper, deseeded and cut into thin slices
- 1 courgette, cut into inch-thick semi circles
- 2 sprigs of rosemary
- 1 sprig of thyme
- 1 tbsp olive oil
- 2 garlic cloves, thinly sliced
- 10 medium eggs
- 100ml semi-skimmed milk
- 20g parmesan, grated
- 5g parsley, roughly chopped
- 60g smoked mackerel, skin removed and broken into small pieces
- 2 x 160g bags Italian-style salad, to serve

DIRECTIONS

1. Line a 30 cm x 20 cm baking dish with baking paper, making sure it overlaps on the sides. Season the vegetables with rosemary, thyme, and olive oil, then place them on the baking sheet. Roast for 15 minutes.
2. Add garlic and roast for another 10 minutes. Remove from the oven, remove the herb stems, and lower the oven to 180°C/160°C *fan*/gas mark 4.
3. Beat eggs with milk, Parmesan cheese, parsley, and seasoning. Spread the smoked mackerel over the vegetables, then pour the egg mixture over them. Bake for 30 minutes (the surface should be golden brown).
4. Allow to cool slightly, then cut into squares and serve with salad leaves.

Nutrition: 340kcal, 20.8g Fat, 3.1g Carbohydrate, 1.1g Fibre, 7.3g Protein

LOW-CARB BEEF STEW

15 minutes

1 hour 30 minutes

4

INGREDIENTS

- 400 g of beef, diced
- 1 tsp salt
- 1 tsp black pepper
- 2 tbsp olive oil
- 400 g of mushroom, sliced
- 1 onion, sliced
- 1 carrot, peeled and cut into small pieces
- 2 stalks celery, sliced
- 2 garlic cloves, peeled and minced
- 4 tbsp tomato paste
- 1 tsp dried mixed herbs
- 4 beef stock cubes

DIRECTIONS

1. Season the beef with salt and pepper.
2. Heat the olive oil in a large saucepan and cook the beef in two batches for 4-5 minutes until cooked and golden. Add more oil if necessary.
3. Add the mushrooms and cook for a further 5 minutes. Add the onion, carrot, celery, garlic, tomato paste, and dried mixed herbs. Stir to combine and coat the vegetables.
4. Crumble the stock cubes into the pan and add 600 ml of boiling water. Bring to a boil before reducing the heat and simmering for 60 minutes.
5. Serve the stew piping hot and enjoy!

Nutrition: 199 kcals, 12 g Fat, 7 g Carbohydrates, 25 g Protein

HUNTER'S CHICKEN

15 minutes   1 hour 15 minutes   4

INGREDIENTS

For the chicken:

- 1 tbsp olive oil
- 45 g black pitted olives
- 850 g chicken, thighs and drumsticks
- 50 g unsmoked bacon medallions, cut into strips
- 500 g passata
- 1 red onion, finely chopped
- 2 garlic cloves, finely chopped
- 150 ml chicken stock made with 1/2 reduced stock cube
- 2 sprigs of rosemary
- 1 bay leaf
- Freshly ground black pepper

For the mash:

- 700 g potatoes, cut into chunks
- 20 g unsalted butter
- Freshly ground black pepper

DIRECTIONS

1. In a medium lidded casserole dish, heat the oil over a medium-high heat on the hob. Brown the chicken for 5-8 minutes, turning so it's golden brown all over. Remove from the pan and set aside.

2. Reduce the heat to medium, and add the bacon to the pan. Fry until starting to crisp, and then add the onion. Fry for another couple of minutes until the onion is starting to soften and then add the garlic, rosemary and bay leaf. Cook for a further minute before returning the chicken to the pan.

3. Add the passata and stock to the casserole. Bring to a gentle simmer over a low heat and then cover. Cook for 1 hour, removing the lid for the last 15 minutes of cooking time. At the end, stir through the olives to warm through. Season with freshly ground black pepper.

4. While the casserole is cooking, make the mashed potato. Put the potatoes in a pan and cover with cold water. Bring to the boil and simmer for around 20 minutes, or until really tender. Remove from the heat, drain and leave the potatoes in the colander for a couple of minutes until most of the steam evaporates. Return to the pan and add the butter. Mash until smooth and season with freshly ground black pepper.

5. Serve the chicken with the mash.

Nutrition: 504kcal, 15.5g Fat, 31.2g Carbohydrate, 2.5g Fibre, 58.7g Protein

STEAK WITH CHIMICHURRI SAUCE

10 minutes

15 minutes

4

INGREDIENTS

- 21-day matured rump steak 225g x4
- 100g fresh flat leaf parsley
- 100g fresh coriander
- 2 tbsp olive oil
- 2 garlic cloves
- 1 onion
- 1 red chilli
- 2 tbsp red wine vinegar
- 300g cherry tomatoes

DIRECTIONS

1. Preheat the oven to 180C. Let the steaks stand at room temperature for 15-20 minutes, season with a little oil and set aside.
2. Blend the herbs, garlic, onion and chili with the oil and vinegar and add salt and pepper to taste.
3. Place the tomatoes in a baking dish, season and add a little oil, then bake for about 5 to 7 minutes.
4. Once the tomatoes are cooked, heat a heavy-bottomed skillet and, once hot, add the steaks. Cook for 2 minutes per side if medium rare, 2 1/2 minutes for medium and 4-5 minutes for well-done. Serve with the Chimichurri sauce and tomatoes on the side.

Nutrition: 656kcal, 46.0g Fat, 6.4g Carbohydrate, 3.0g Fibre, 51.0g Protein

FAJITA CHICKEN

15 minutes

30 minutes

4

INGREDIENTS

- 1 tbsp paprika
- 1 tbsp chili powder
- 1 tsp dried chives
- 2 tsp cumin
- 1 tsp salt
- 1 tsp black pepper
- 200 g of skinless, boneless chicken breast, sliced
- 1 red pepper, sliced
- 1 yellow pepper, sliced
- 1 onion, sliced
- 2 garlic cloves, peeled and minced
- 2 tbsp olive oil
- 1 tbsp lime juice
- 1 tbsp salsa
- 1 tbsp guacamole

DIRECTIONS

1. Preheat the oven to 180 °C and line a baking tray with parchment paper.
2. Mix the paprika, chili powder, dried chives, cumin, salt, and black pepper in a bowl. Set aside.
3. In a separate bowl, mix the chicken breast, peppers, onion, garlic, olive oil, and lime juice together. Toss to coat the chicken and vegetables in the oil.
4. Spread the chicken and vegetables evenly across the lined baking tray and cook for 25-30 minutes until the chicken is golden and tender, and the vegetables are soft.
5. Remove from the oven and serve with the spices, salsa, and guacamole on top.

Nutrition: 411 kcals, 15 g Carbohydrates, 21 g Protein, 14 g Fat

PLANT PIONEERS BUBBLE AND SQUEAK CAKES

15 minutes

25 minutes

2

INGREDIENTS

- 2 packs Plant Pioneers mash potato
- 225 g cooked greens or frozen peas, defrosted
- 1 tbsp olive oil
- 0.5 large leek, thinly sliced
- 2 tbsp plain flour
- 1 tsp white wine vinegar
- Vegan butter - to cook with

For the mustard sauce:
- 150 ml vegetable stock or light chicken stock
- 2.5 tbsp dry white wine
- 2 tbsp plant based double cream
- 25 g vegan butter, plus 1 extra tsp
- 0.5 tsp plain flour
- 1 tsp wholegrain mustard

DIRECTIONS

1. Be sure to dry both the potatoes and vegetables well to ensure that the cakes become crispy. If using vegetables, cut them into small pieces.

2. Heat 1/2 of the vegan butter in a small skillet. Add the sliced leek and cook for 3 minutes, stirring until lightly browned. Mix *together* the cooked leek, mashed potatoes, vegetables, and seasoning in a bowl, add flour to firm up the mixture, and form 4 disks about 2.5 cm thick.

3. Heat the remaining vegan butter in a nonstick skillet. Fry the cupcakes over medium heat for 4-5 minutes on each side until crisp and golden brown.

4. Cook the asparagus on the griddle for a few minutes on each side until cooked through and serve along with the cakes.

Nutrition: 360kcal, 14.0g Fat, 43.0g Carbohydrate, 11.0g Fibre, 9.6g Protein

PARSNIP AND APPLE SOUP

5 minutes

35 minutes

10

INGREDIENTS

- 2 tsp olive oil
- 1 large onion, chopped
- 700 g parsnips, peeled and roughly chopped
- 250 g potatoes, peeled and roughly chopped
- 2 Braeburn apples, peeled and roughly chopped
- 0.5 tsp dried rosemary
- 2 very low-salt vegetable stock cubes
- 250 ml whole milk

DIRECTIONS

1. Heat the oil in a large pot, add the onion and cook for 5 minutes or until soft. Add the parsnips, potatoes, apples and rosemary and stir to heat through. Prepare 1 liter of stock, pour it into the saucepan and bring it to the boil. Cover and cook for 25 minutes (the vegetables should become tender).
2. With an immersion blender, reduce the soup to a puree until it has a velvety consistency. Add the milk and heat up.

Nutrition: 106kcal, 2.4g Fat, 16.1g Carbohydrate, 3.8g Fibre, 3.1g Protein

CHICKEN, ALMONDS, AND GRAPES

10 minutes

35 minutes

4

INGREDIENTS

- 100 g whole blanched almonds
- 4 tbsp olive oil
- 6 garlic cloves, unpeeled
- 1 kg free-range chicken thighs and drumsticks
- 2 tsp sherry vinegar
- 30 white seedless grapes

DIRECTIONS

1. Toast 6 almonds in a large frying pan until golden brown. Remove the almonds, cut them into slivers and set them aside. Add the olive oil to the frying pan and heat it up, then add the garlic cloves and fry for 3 minutes, turning once. Once the oil has seasoned remove the garlic.
2. Salt the chicken and add it to the pan with the skin side down. Fry gently for 5-10 minutes until the skin is golden brown and quite crispy. Be careful of oil splattering.
3. Meanwhile, chop the remaining almonds as finely as possible in the blender. Then, with the blender still running, slowly add the vinegar and then 200 ml water, a little at a time, until smooth and creamy. Set aside.
4. Cut the grapes in half. Turn the chicken, add the previously fried garlic and the grapes and cook for half a minute. Then add the almond mixture. Cover and let the chicken cook in the sauce for 15-20 minutes. If the sauce becomes too thick, add a little water.
5. Check the seasoning and sprinkle the chicken with chopped almonds. Serve with a dressed green salad or purple broccoli, if desired.

Nutrition: 561kcal, 41.2g Fat, 8.4g Carbohydrate, 3.0g Fibre, 37.6g Protein

GREEK SALAD

10 minutes

0 minutes

6

INGREDIENTS

- 200g 50% less fat Greek-style cheese, cut into bite-size pieces
- 8 vine tomatoes, washed and cut into wedges
- 150g Greek kalamata olives
- 1 red onion, finely sliced
- 3 tbsp extra virgin olive oil
- 2 tbsp freshly squeezed lemon juice
- ½ tsp cayenne pepper
- ½ tsp caster sugar

DIRECTIONS

1. In a large bowl, mix together the feta, tomatoes, olives and red onion.
2. Combine the olive oil, lemon juice, cayenne pepper and sugar in a small bowl and season with freshly ground black pepper. Drizzle over the salad just before serving.

Nutrition: 191kcal, Fat 16.4g, 4.0g Carbohydrate, 1.4g Fibre, 6.4g Protein

CHICKEN CAESAR SALAD

10 minutes

8 minutes

4

INGREDIENTS

- 2 tablespoons of olive oil
- 25 g of Parmesan
- 4 chicken breasts
- 4 eggs
- 1 Romaine lettuce
- 3 tablespoons of lemon juice
- 170 g of fat free Greek yoghurt / yogurt
- 50 g of anchovy fillets
- 50 g oz of watercress

DIRECTIONS

1. Boil 4 eggs until fully cooked and then cool, peel, and rinse. Cut into quarters.
2. Chop half of the anchovies and grate the Parmesan, and then mix these together with yoghurt / yogurt and lemon juice. Taste and alter the quantities if necessary.
3. Add the chicken breasts, lettuce, cress, egg quarters, and the yoghurt / yogurt mixture to a bowl, and top the salad with the remaining whole anchovies and enjoy.

Nutrition: 461 kcal, 20.8 g Fat, 8 g Carbohydrate, 0.2 g Fibre, 59 g Protein

HOT AND SPICY SHRIMP LETTUCE WRAPS

15 minutes

5 minutes

4

INGREDIENTS

- 400 g of shrimp, peeled, deveined, and tails removed
- 1 tbsp hot sauce
- 1 tbsp olive oil
- 1 head lettuce, separated into large leaves
- ½ red onion, finely sliced
- 4 cherry tomatoes, halved
- 50 g of cheddar cheese, grated

DIRECTIONS

1. Place the shrimp in a bowl and toss in the hot sauce.
2. Heat 1 tbsp olive in a pan and add the shrimp. Cook for 2-3 minutes on each side.
3. Assemble the wraps by placing the large lettuce leaves on a plate. Evenly spread the cooked shrimp between the leaves before topping with chopped onion, halved cherry tomatoes, and grated cheddar cheese.
4. Add a dash of extra hot sauce if desired and enjoy!

Nutrition: 225 kcal, 8 g Fat, 4 g Carbohydrates, 12 g Protein

MEDITERRANEAN MACKEREL SALAD

15 minutes

0 minutes

6

INGREDIENTS

- 2 tins of mackerel in sunflower oil
- ½ red onion
- 1/3 cup of parsley
- 2 teaspoons of capers
- 30 g of feta cheese
- 1 cucumber
- ½ avocado
- 410 g of tinned chickpeas (drain and rinse)
- ¼ teaspoon of black pepper
- Pinch of salt
- 150 g of roasted red peppers

To make the vinaigrette:

- 2 tablespoons of red wine vinegar
- 2 tablespoons of olive oil
- 1 teaspoon of oregano
- 1 teaspoon of parsley
- 1 teaspoon of lemon juice
- ¼ teaspoon of black pepper

DIRECTIONS

1. Drain your mackerel and tip it into a large bowl.
2. Wash and chop your cucumber, red peppers, parsley, red onion, and avocado, and crumble the feta cheese.
3. Add all of the ingredients to the mackerel's bowl and stir to combine.
4. To make the vinaigrette, in a separate bowl, whisk together chopped parsley and oregano, lemon juice, black pepper, salt, olive oil, and red wine vinegar. Taste and adjust if necessary, and then drizzle generously across your salad.

Nutrition: 291 kcal, 17 g Fat, 24.2 g Carbohydrate, 5.7 g Fibre, 12.6 g Protein

SALMON, POTATO, AND LEEK BAKE

| 15 minutes | 30 minutes | 2 |

INGREDIENTS

- 2 tablespoons of olive oil
- 1 clove of garlic
- 2 salmon fillets
- 70 ml of double cream / heavy cream
- 1 leek
- 1 tablespoon of chives
- 1 tablespoon of capers
- 50 g of rocket / arugula
- 250 g of baby potatoes
- 75 ml of hot water

Nutrition: 588 kcal, 38.6 g Fat, 24.5 g Carbohydrate, 4.5 g Fibre, 40 g Protein

DIRECTIONS

1. Preheat your oven to 200 degrees C.
2. Wash your potatoes and bring a pan of water to the boil while you cut them into thick slices. Add the slices to the pan and boil for about 8 minutes.
3. Drain the potatoes and leave them to dry for a few minutes, and then tip them into a baking dish and toss them with a tablespoon of olive oil and some seasoning.
4. Put the potatoes in the oven for 10 minutes and then take them out and toss them again, and put them back for another 10 minutes.
5. While the potatoes are cooking, add the remaining tablespoon of olive oil to a large skillet. Wash the leek and slice it into thin strips, and then fry it for several minutes until it starts to soften.
6. Crush your garlic and stir it in with the leek, and then add the capers, the cream, and the hot water. Bring it to a gentle boil, making sure it doesn't stick, and stir in some chopped chives.
7. Put your grill on a high heat. Take the potatoes out of the oven and pour your leeks and cream over them, stirring gently to combine. Place the salmon fillets on top and then grill for around 8 minutes, until the salmon reaches an internal temperature of at least 60 degrees C, and the flesh is flaky and tender.
8. Top with extra chives and capers, and serve with the washed rocket / arugula.

STUFFED AVOCADOS

10 minutes

5 minutes

2

INGREDIENTS

- 2 medium avocados
- 2 slices bacon
- 4 cherry tomatoes, halved
- 1 tsp lemon or lime juice
- ½ tsp garlic powder
- ½ tsp black pepper

DIRECTIONS

1. Heat a skillet and add the bacon slices. Cook for 5 minutes on either side until the edges begin to curl and the bacon begins to brown and turn crispy.
2. Once cooked, set the bacon aside to drain on some paper towels.
3. Peel the avocadoes, and slice down the middle so that each one forms two even halves. Remove the pits, trying to keep each avocado untouched.
4. Slice the cooked bacon into small pieces and place in a bowl. Add the halved cherry tomatoes, 1 tsp lemon or lime juice, and garlic powder. Mix to combine.
5. Spoon the mixture into the holes of each avocado half and sprinkle some black pepper over the top of each.

Nutrition: 112 kcal, 8 g Carbohydrates, 6 g Protein, 12 g Fat

CHICKEN WITH PESTO VEGGIES

5 minutes

15 minutes

4

INGREDIENTS

- 115 g of pesto
- 455 g of green beans
- 2 tablespoons of olive oil
- 400 g of cherry tomatoes
- 4 boneless, skinless chicken thighs
- Pinch of salt
- Pinch of pepper

DIRECTIONS

1. Heat the oil in a large skillet and add the chicken thighs, plus seasoning. Cook until the chicken is fully done and has reached an internal temperature of 75 degrees C.
2. Set the chicken aside to cool and then slice it into thin strips.
3. Add the green beans to the pan and cook until they turn tender, and then toss the chicken back in too. Stir in the pesto.
4. Wash and halve your cherry tomatoes and add these to the pan. Stir well so the ingredients are fully mixed and then turn off the heat and serve the meal, or chill in the fridge.

Nutrition: 634 kcal, 25.4 g Fat, 12.1 g Carbohydrate, 5.1 g Fibre, 91 g Protein

LEMONY CHICKEN AND AVOCADO SALAD

8 minutes

10 minutes

6

INGREDIENTS

- 2 medium avocados
- 3 teaspoons of mayonnaise
- 420 g of cooked chicken
- 40 g of spring onion / green onion
- 2 teaspoons of chopped coriander / cilantro
- 3 teaspoons of lemon juice
- Pinch of salt

DIRECTIONS

1. Cut your cooked chicken into large chunks and then dice the avocados and add both ingredients to a large mixing bowl with 1 teaspoon of lemon juice and a little salt.
2. Peel and dice your spring onion / green onion and chop the coriander / cilantro.
3. Mix the remaining lemon juice with the mayonnaise and taste. Adjust the flavour if necessary.
4. Add the onions and dressing to the chicken and avocado and toss the mixture thoroughly until the chicken and avocado are coated. Gently stir in the coriander / cilantro.
5. Chill and then serve cold.

Nutrition: 254 kcal, 16.1 g Fat, 6.8 g Carbohydrate, 4.7 g Fibre, 21.7 g Protein

AUBERGINE / EGGPLANT PIZZA

10 minutes

20 minutes

6

INGREDIENTS

- 1 aubergine / eggplant
- 80 ml of olive oil
- 280 g of marinara sauce
- ½ a red pepper
- 400 g of tomatoes
- 115 g of mozzarella
- 3 teaspoons of fresh basil
- Pinch of salt
- Pinch of pepper
-

DIRECTIONS

1. Preheat your oven to 200 degrees C.
2. Wash your aubergine / eggplant and remove the ends, and then slice into 2 cm rounds. Place the slices on a tray and brush both sides generously with olive oil, and then season.
3. Place them in the oven and roast for about 11 minutes until they start to become tender.
4. Wash and halve your tomatoes and wash and slice the red pepper.
5. Take the aubergine / eggplant out of the oven and top it with marinara sauce.
6. Add the tomatoes and red pepper, and then sprinkle grated mozzarella across the top.
7. Roast for another 6 minutes, until the cheese is melting and the tomatoes and peppers are cooked.
8. Serve hot with a sprinkling of basil and extra salt or pepper if you like.

Nutrition: 207 kcal, 14.4 g Fat, 17.3 g Carbohydrate, 5.7 g Fibre, 4.7 g Protein

MAC AND CHEESE WITH CAULIFLOWER

5 minutes

40 minutes

8

INGREDIENTS

- ½ teaspoon of butter
- 2 tablespoons of olive oil
- 170 g cream cheese
- 450 g cheddar cheese
- 450 g of mozzarella cheese
- 240 ml double cream / heavy cream
- Pinch of black pepper
- Pinch of salt
- 2 medium cauliflowers

DIRECTIONS

1. Preheat your oven to 190 degrees C and use the butter to grease a large baking dish.
2. Wash your cauliflowers and chop them into florets.
3. Add the florets to a large bowl and toss them with the oil and a little salt.
4. Spread the cauliflower onto 2 baking sheets and put it in the oven to roast until tender (about 40 minutes).
5. Grate the cheddar and mozzarella cheeses.
6. In a large pan, heat the cream over a medium heat. Simmer gently and then lower the heat and stir in the cheeses, including the cream cheese. Keep stirring gently until they have fully melted.
7. Remove from the heat and season and then fold in the roasted cauliflower.
8. Tip the mixture into your baking dish and if you wish to add any toppings to your mac and cheese (e.g. extra cheese, dried herbs, etc.), do so.
9. Put back in the oven and bake for 15 minutes, until golden, and then serve hot.

Nutrition: 312 kcal, 22.1 g Fat, 10 g Carbohydrate, 3.6 g Fibre, 20.5 g Protein

SCALLOPS AND TOMATOES IN BUTTER

5 minutes

10 minutes

4

INGREDIENTS

- 1 tablespoon of extra-virgin olive oil
- 400 g of cherry tomatoes
- 120 ml of dry white wine
- ¼ teaspoon of black pepper
- 2 tablespoons of capers
- 3 tablespoons of butter
- 450 g of dry sea scallops (remove the muscle)
- 10 g fresh parsley

DIRECTIONS

1. Heat the oil in a large skillet over a medium heat. Pat your scallops dry and add them to the pan, cooking for a couple of minutes. Flip them over and cook them for another 2-3 minutes until they are golden. Put them in a bowl with a lid and set them aside.

2. Wash your cherry tomatoes and add them to the pan, gently cooking them until they start to turn brown and burst open.

3. Rinse your capers and add them to the pan, followed by the wine. Cook until the mixture has reduced by half, which should take a couple of minutes.

4. Take the pan off the heat, add the pepper, and then stir in the butter.

5. Serve the scallops with the sauce drizzled across the top and a garnishing of chopped parsley.

Nutrition: 249 kcal, 13.2 g Fat, 7.4 g Carbohydrate, 1.3 g Fibre, 20.1 g Protein

DELICIOUS SALMON BURGERS

10 minutes

10 minutes

4

INGREDIENTS

- 1 tablespoon of Thai red curry paste
- 1 teaspoon of soy sauce
- 30 g of coriander / cilantro
- 1 teaspoon of vegetable oil
- 550 g of salmon fillets (skinless, boneless)
- 1 thumb of ginger (approx. 25 g)
- 4 lemon wedges

DIRECTIONS

1. If you have a food processor, use it to chop and mix the salmon, soy sauce, ginger, Thai red curry paste and coriander / cilantro. If you don't have a food processor, chop the salmon by hand and mix it thoroughly with the grated ginger, chopped coriander / cilantro, soy sauce, and Thai red curry paste. You should get a thick mixture.
2. Tip this onto a clean surface and shape it into four burgers.
3. Add oil to a non-stick skillet and warm over a medium heat, and then fry the burgers for around 5 minutes. Flip them and fry for another 5 minutes, until they are crispy and hot through.
4. Serve piping hot or space out to cool and freeze.

Nutrition: 84 kcal, 4.7 g Fat, 7 g Carbohydrate, 1.2 g Fibre, 3.6 g Protein

BACON SUSHI ROLLS

10 minutes

20 minutes

8

INGREDIENTS

- 1 tbsp olive oil
- 4 slices bacon
- 1 cucumber
- 2 carrots,
- 1 avocado
- 100 g of cream cheese

DIRECTIONS

1. Heat the olive oil in a skillet and cook the bacon for 4-5 minutes until crispy and brown. Set aside to drain on paper towels.
2. Cut the cucumber, carrots, and avocado into thin strips that are the same width and thickness as the bacon slices.
3. Spread a layer of cream cheese along each strip of bacon and layer with cucumber, carrot, and avocado slices. Repeat until all of the vegetables are used.
4. Roll each slice of bacon up tightly into a sushi roll and serve warm or cold.

Nutrition: 112 kcal, 15 g Fat, 6 g Carbohydrates, 8 g Protein

CAULIFLOWER POTATO SALAD

5 minutes

10 minutes

4

INGREDIENTS

- 1 large cauliflower, broken into florets
- 2 eggs
- 1 tbsp mayonnaise
- 1 tbsp olive oil
- 1 tsp Dijon mustard
- 1 tsp white vinegar
- 1 tsp cumin
- 1 tsp smoked paprika
- ½ tsp salt
- ½ tsp black pepper
- ½ red onion, sliced

DIRECTIONS

1. Bring a saucepan of water to boil and add the cauliflower. Cook for 8-10 minutes until softened. Drain and set aside to cool slightly.
2. Meanwhile, heat a second pan of water to a simmer and add the eggs. Cook for 10 minutes to create hardboiled eggs. Set aside to cool before peeling the eggs and slicing them in half.
3. In a bowl combine, the remaining ingredients. Add the cauliflower to the bowl and toss to fully coat.
4. Evenly spread the cauliflower between 4 bowls and add half a hard-boiled egg to each.

Nutrition: 257 kcals, 8 g Carbohydrates, 6 g Protein, 12 g Fat

CHOCO NUT BITES

15 minutes

10 minutes

25

INGREDIENTS

- 120 g unsalted English butter
- 125 ml semi-skimmed milk
- 225 g Fairtrade white granulated sugar
- 50 g cocoa powder
- 300 g porridge oats
- 100 g pistachios, deshelled and crushed
- 1 tsp vanilla extract
- 100 g desiccated coconut

DIRECTIONS

1. Melt together the butter and milk in a saucepan over a medium heat. Combine the sugar and cocoa, then add to the milk and cook for 5 minutes, or until the sugar has completely dissolved.
2. Remove from the heat and stir in the oats, pistachios, vanilla extract and half the coconut.
3. Sprinkle the remaining coconut over a plate and drop spoonfuls of the mixture into the coconut; roll into balls to coat. Transfer to a tray lined with baking parchment, then chill in the fridge for 15 minutes to set.

Nutrition: 168kcal, 9.6g Fat, 42.0g Carbohydrate, 6.5g Fibre, 8.3g Protein

CRANBERRY CRÈME BRÛLÉES

| 15 minutes | 1 hour 20 minutes | 6 |

INGREDIENTS

For the cranberry compote:
- 250 g cranberries
- a few strips of pared orange zest, plus extra zest to serve
- 50 g caster sugar

For the custard:
- 6 medium egg yolks
- 3 tbsp heaped caster sugar
- 1 vanilla pod, split lengthways, seeds removed
- 600 ml double cream
- 1 tbsp icing sugar, for dusting
- For the caramel:
- 125 g caster sugar

You will also need:
- 6 x 150ml glass ramekins

Nutrition: 168kcal, 9.6g Fat, 42.0g Carbohydrate, 6.5g Fibre, 8.3g Protein

DIRECTIONS

1. For the compote, place the cranberries in a saucepan with the orange zest and cook gently over a low heat for 5-8 minutes. Add the 50 g caster sugar and heat for a few more minutes, stirring occasionally, until the sugar has dissolved and blended with the juice. Now transfer to a bowl, remove the orange peel and leave to cool.

2. Blend all the ingredients for the custard, except the icing sugar, and sieve them into a bowl or jug. Divide a little less than half of the mixture between the ramekins, then divide the whole custard mixture between them. Place in a pan with hot but not boiling water reaching two thirds of the way up the sides of the ramekins and bake for about 1 hour or until lightly browned and cooked through. By moving a ramekin from side to side, the custard should wobble, but there should be no trace of liquid under the surface. Remove the ramekins from the baking tray and allow them to cool to room temperature.

3. Gently heat the sugar for the caramel in a saucepan until about half has liquefied and started to colour, then stir. Keep an eye on the caramel, stirring often, until it turns deep gold, then remove from the heat. Dust the surface of each cream with icing sugar, using a tea strainer, then pour a teaspoon of caramel over it. The caramel should harden in a few minutes. Cover and chill in the refrigerator for a couple of hours.

4. Top with the remaining compote and orange zest

RHUBARB AND CUSTARD MUFFINS

15 minutes

45 minutes

12

INGREDIENTS

- 400g rhubarb, trimmed
- 140g light brown sugar
- 75ml vegetable oil
- 1 large free-range egg
- 1 orange, zested
- 300g self-raising flour
- 300ml soured cream
- 120ml fresh custard
- 2 tsp icing sugar, to dust

DIRECTIONS

1. Preheat the oven to 200°C/fan 180°C/gas mark 6. Cut the rhubarb into 5cm lengths. Place in a shallow roasting tin so they sit in one layer. Add 50g of the sugar and turn the rhubarb to coat well.
2. Cover the tin with foil and bake for 15 minutes until the rhubarb is tender but still retains its shape. Leave to cool.
3. Meanwhile, mix together the remaining sugar, oil, egg and orange zest in a bowl, but be careful not to over beat. Stir through the flour and cream, then gently fold in the rhubarb. Divide the mixture between a 12-hole muffin tin lined with paper cases. Bake for 20-25 minutes (they should be risen and golden).
4. Cool for 10 minutes, then cut a small deep cross in the top of each muffin and spoon on 1 tsp custard. Leave to settle before adding another 1 tsp custard on top. Dust with icing sugar and serve warm.

Nutrition: 236 kcal, 11.0g Fat, 30.7g Carbohydrate, 1.3g Fibre, 3.5g Protein

CHOCOLATE AND BANANA MOLTEN CAKES

15 minutes

40 minutes

4

INGREDIENTS

For the hazelnut and date sauce

- 100g dates
- 20g hazelnuts
- 125ml hazelnut milk

For the chocolate and banana cakes

- 100g sunflower spread, plus extra for greasing
- 100g dark chocolate, suitable for vegans, broken into pieces
- 150g caster sugar
- 2 medium bananas, broken into pieces
- ½ tsp vanilla extract
- 75g self-raising flour

DIRECTIONS

1. Soak the dates and hazelnuts in boiling water for 30 minutes. Drain, tip into a food processor, add the hazelnut milk and whizz until smooth. Pass through a sieve into a bowl and set aside.
2. Meanwhile, preheat the oven to 200°C/gas mark 6. Grease four 200ml ramekins with the sunflower spread and line their bases with baking paper.
3. Melt the chocolate and the spread in a small saucepan over a low heat, then pour into a food processor.
4. Add the caster sugar, bananas, vanilla extract and self-raising flour to the food processor and whizz well to combine. Divide the mixture between the four ramekins and bake in the oven for 15 minutes.
5. Run a small knife around the edges of each ramekin, then tip each one on to a small plate. Pour over the sauce and serve immediately.

Nutrition: 596kcal, 24.4g Fat, 86.8g Carbohydrate, 2.9g Fibre, 5.9g Protein

VEGAN ESPRESSO CHOCOLATE MOUSSE

15 minutes

5 minutes

6

INGREDIENTS

- 400g coconut milk
- 200g dairy-free dark chocolate
- 400g chickpeas
- 2 tbsp agave
- 1 tbsp vodka
- 2 tbsp coffee liqueur
- 1 tsp cocoa powder, to decorate

DIRECTIONS

1. Put the coconut milk in the fridge and chill overnight.
2. Melt the chocolate in a bowl over hot water or in the microwave. Leave to cool slightly.
3. Drain the chickpeas and put the liquid into the bowl of a free-standing mixer. Whisk until it forms soft peaks. Add the melted chocolate, agave, vodka and coffee liqueur and stir gently to combine. Divide between 6 martini glasses. Chill in the fridge for a couple of hours, or until set.
4. Drain the liquid from the coconut milk and put the solids in the bowl of a free-standing mixer. Whisk until it has the consistency of whipped cream. Decorate the top of the mousses with the cream. Dust with cocoa powder, if desired.

Nutrition: 319kcal, 21.2g Fat, 25.9g Carbohydrate, 2.5g Fibre, 1.9g Protein

BASQUE CHEESECAKE

10 minutes

1 hour

12

INGREDIENTS

- 650g low fat cream cheese, softened
- 220g caster sugar
- 300ml double cream
- 2 tsp vanilla extract
- A pinch of salt
- 4 large eggs, room temperature, whisked
- 1-2 tbsp icing sugar (optional)

DIRECTIONS

1. Preheat the oven to 200°C and line a 20 cm springform cake tin with a large circle of baking paper, making sure that the paper goes over the edge on the sides.
2. Beat the cream cheese with the sugar, cream, vanilla and salt until smooth. Add the eggs and mix until incorporated.
3. Pour into the prepared baking tin and tap gently on the work surface to remove any air bubbles. Bake for about 50 minutes, until the surface is golden brown. If necessary, increase the oven temperature to 230°C and bake for 10 minutes to brown further. Cool completely and store in the fridge. If desired, dust with icing sugar to serve.

Nutrition: 269 kcal, 17.5 g Fat, 24.0 g Carbohydrate, 0.0 g Fibre, 11.0 g Protein

BLUEBERRY MUFFINS

5 minutes

20 minutes

12

INGREDIENTS

- 3 eggs
- 1 tablespoon of coconut flour
- 1 teaspoon of baking powder
- 2 tablespoons of coconut oil
- 1 tablespoon of vanilla extract
- 1 teaspoon of lemon zest
- 2 tablespoons of lemon juice
- 170 g of almond flour
- 250 g of honey
- ½ teaspoon of salt
- 140 g of blueberries

DIRECTIONS

1. Preheat the oven to 175 degrees C.
2. Take out a large mixing bowl and sift together the coconut flour, almond flour, salt, and baking powder.
3. In a second bowl, whisk together the honey, vanilla extract, coconut oil (melted), lemon juice, lemon zest, and eggs.
4. Tip a little of the honey and egg mixture into the flour mixture and stir until fully combined. Keep gradually adding the honey and eggs and mixing thoroughly until you have a smooth, runny batter.
5. Wash the blueberries and fold them into the mixture, and then grease your muffin trays and pour some mixture into each hole.
6. Bake for about 20 minutes and then use a toothpick to check whether they are cooked through. Serve warm or enjoy cold.

Nutrition: 196 kcal, 10.1 g Fat, 2 g Fibre, 4.6 g Protein

CHOCOLATE MOUSSE

10 minutes

10 minutes

4

INGREDIENTS

- 200 ml whipping cream
- 4 tbsp cocoa powder
- 2 tbsp stevia
- 1 tsp vanilla extract
- 1 tsp cinnamon

DIRECTIONS

1. Whisk the whipping cream into stiff peaks.
2. Fold in the cocoa powder, stevia, vanilla extract, and cinnamon until fully combined.
3. Serve cold as a snack or after dinner.

Nutrition: 219 kcal, 19 g Fat, 10 g Carbohydrates, 8 g Protein,

14 DAYS MEAL-PLAN

DAY 1
Breakfast: Vegan pancakes p.11

Lunch: Seafood stew with paprika p.34

Dinner: Greek salad p.49

Dessert: Rhubarb and custard muffins p.65

DAY 2
Breakfast: Goji berry and chia seed bowl p.18

Lunch: Fajita Chicken p.45

Dinner: Aubergine / Eggplant Pizza p.57

Dessert: Vegan espresso chocolate mousse p.67

DAY 3
Breakfast: Low-Carb Breakfast Waffles p.21

Lunch: Cheddar and leek croquettes p.38

Dinner: Roast vegetable frittata with mackerel p.41

Dessert: Cranberry crème brûlées p.64

DAY 4
Breakfast: Baked Egg Avocados p.16

Lunch: Bacon Sushi Rolls p.61

Dinner: Baked orzo with graffiti aubergine p.32

Dessert: Choco nut bites p.63

DAY 5
Breakfast: Kefir pancakes p.13

Lunch: Chicken, almonds, and grapes p.48

Dinner: Mac and Cheese with Cauliflower p.58

Dessert: Blueberry Muffins p.69

DAY 6
Breakfast: Bacon and Egg Rolls p.17

Lunch: Steak with Chimichurri sauce p.44

Dinner: Delicious Salmon Burgers p.60

Dessert: Chocolate Mousse p.70

DAY 7
Breakfast: Scrambled Eggs and Smoked Salmon p.20

Lunch: Greek salad p.49

Dinner: Hunter's chicken p.43

Dessert: Basque cheesecake p.68

DAY 8

Breakfast: Banana Bread p.22

Lunch: Cauliflower Potato Salad p.62

Dinner: Sausage and roasted vegetable couscous p.37

Dessert: Vegan espresso chocolate mousse p.67

DAY 9

Breakfast: Avocado Toast p.14

Lunch: Chicken Caesar Salad p.50

Dinner: Baked orzo with graffiti aubergine p.32

Dessert: Chocolate and banana molten cakes p.66

DAY 10

Breakfast: Scrambled eggs with porcini and prosciutto p.15

Lunch: Greek lamb wraps p.39

Dinner: Plant Pioneers bubble and squeak cakes p.46

Dessert: Rhubarb and custard muffins p.65

DAY 11

Breakfast: Vegan pancakes p.11

Lunch: Sausage and roasted vegetable couscous p.37

Dinner: Lemony Chicken and Avocado Salad p.56

Dessert: Blueberry Muffins p.69

DAY 12

Breakfast: Caramelized banana bread waffles p.12

Lunch: Stuffed Avocados p.54

Dinner: Mediterranean Mackerel Salad p.52

Dessert: Choco nut bites p.63

DAY 13

Breakfast: Low-Carb Breakfast Waffles p.21

Lunch: Jamaican-style coconut fish parcels p.40

Dinner: Scallops and Tomatoes in Butter p.59

Dessert: Chocolate Mousse p.70

DAY 14

Breakfast: Baked Egg Avocados p.16

Lunch: Seafood stew with paprika p.34

Dinner: Cheddar and leek croquettes p.38

Dessert: Basque cheesecake p.68

CONVERSION TABLE

Volume Equivalents (Liquid)

US STANDARD
US STANDARD (OUNCES)
METRIC (APPROXIMATE)

2 tbsp
1 fl. oz.
30 mL

1/4 cup
2 fl. oz.
60 mL

1/2 cup
4 fl. oz.
120 mL

1 cup
8 fl. oz.
240 mL

11/2 cups
12 fl. oz.
355 mL

2 cups or 1 pint
16 fl. oz.
475 mL

4 cups or 1 quart
32 fl. oz.
1 L

1 gallon
128 fl. oz.
4 L

Volume Equivalents (Dry)

US STANDARD
METRIC (APPROXIMATE)

1/8 tsp
0.5 mL

1/4 tsp
1 mL

1/2 tsp
2 mL

3/4 tsp
4 mL

1 tsp
5 mL

1 tbsp
15 mL

1/4 cup
59 mL

1/3 cup
79 mL

1/2 cup
118 mL

2/3 cup	**300°F**
156 mL	150°C
3/4 cup	**325°F**
177 mL	165°C
1 cup	**350°F**
235 mL	180°C
2 cups or 1 pint	**375°F**
475 mL	190°C
3 cups	**400°F**
700 mL	200°C
4 cups or 1 quart	**425°F**
1 L	220°C

Oven Temperatures

	450°F
FAHRENHEIT (F)	230°C
CELSIUS (C) (APPROXIMATE)	
250°F	
120°C	

INDEX

CREDITS

Icon made by Pixel perfect from www.flaticon.com

Printed in Great Britain
by Amazon